PUFFIN BOOKS

MAD MYTHS:
MIND THE DOOR!

Steve Barlow was born in Crewe. He has been a refuse collector, laundry-van driver, postal worker and puppeteer. He spent four years teaching English in a village school in Botswana, where a valid excuse for not having your homework was: 'A goat ate it, sir!'

He currently teaches performing arts at a college in Nottingham. He lives in Derbyshire with his wife, two children and a cat called Captain Birdseye. He enjoys sailing, walking, listening to music and shouting at politicians on the telly.

Steve Skidmore was born in Leicestershire. He has never been to Crewe. He is younger and much shorter than Steve Barlow. The first fact annoys Barlow, but Skidmore doesn't go on about it because of the second.

He has had a variety of jobs, including one that involved counting pastry lids on meat pies. He has not eaten a meat pie since. He enjoys most sports, especially Rugby Union, and supports Leicester Tigers.

Steve Barlow and Steve Skidmore have written quite a few books together, including the *Mad Myths* series.

SURFERS

Mad Myths

MIND THE DOOR!

Steve Barlow & Steve Skidmore

Illustrated by
Tony Ross

PUFFIN BOOKS

PUFFIN BOOKS

Published by the Penguin Group
Penguin Books Ltd, 27 Wrights Lane, London W8 5TZ, England
Penguin Putnam Inc., 375 Hudson Street, New York, New York 10014, USA
Penguin Books Australia Ltd, Ringwood, Victoria, Australia
Penguin Books Canada Ltd, 10 Alcorn Avenue, Toronto, Ontario, Canada M4V 3B2
Penguin Books (NZ) Ltd, 182–190 Wairau Road, Auckland 10, New Zealand

Penguin Books Ltd, Registered Offices: Harmondsworth, Middlesex, England

First published by Hamish Hamilton 1996
Published in Puffin Books 1997
5 7 9 10 8 6 4

Text copyright © Steve Barlow & Steve Skidmore, 1996
Illustrations copyright © Tony Ross, 1996
All rights reserved

Filmset in Bembo

Made and printed in England by Clays Ltd. St Ives plc

British Library Cataloguing in Publication Data
A CIP catalogue record for this book is available from the British Library

ISBN 0-140-37725-5

Contents

Mind the Door!

THE CELLAR DOOR stood at the bottom of a flight of worn concrete steps guarded by painted iron railings, behind the school kitchen. For years, nobody had given it a second glance.

When the school was heated by solid fuel, it was different. Then, the cellar door had led to a world of fire and smoke. The two boilers, hunched and massive, sat groaning like chained beasts. The red glow from their fireboxes had

1

made the small cellar into a terrible Underworld, full of the flames and roar of molten lava. You could imagine a demon king and his imps leaping around bent on mischief, and even hear the shrieks of lost souls, though the caretaker said that was just air in the pipes.

These days the boilers were timid little boxes that ran quietly on North Sea gas. The cellar had become the maintenance store, home to buckets, mops, disinfectant and rolls of scratchy lavatory paper (special schools issue) and paper towels. The magic of the cellar had gone, and the wooden door with its small panes of frosted glass and peeling green paint was . . . just another door.

But doors are chancy things. When you go through a door, you go from *here* to *there,* and usually the place you end up in is the place you expected to get to.

But not always.

Hidden away in its quiet corner of the school yard, the cellar door waited.

Chapter One
Take Care, Caretaker!

"PARENTS. WHO'D HAVE them?" growled Perce. She kicked a stray ball back into a mêlée of kids trying to kill each other.

"Actually, I think they had you. You see, when a mummy loves a daddy very, very much . . ." Andy tailed off as Perce fixed her "look" on him. "Tell you what, I'll shut up."

"Like this morning," complained Perce, ignoring Andy, "I'm trying to get ready for school when Mum starts on me: 'Have you

3

cleaned your room yet?' She knows I haven't. So why ask? What she's really saying is: 'Go and tidy your bedroom now!' "

Andy nodded. "My mum says things like that as well. Before tea she *always* asks me: 'Have you washed your hands?' She knows I never have."

"Exactly! What she's really saying is: 'Go and wash them!' So when I pointed out to Mum what she was really saying, she said I was being cheeky. Then Dad joined in and that led to a big row and now I've been grounded until I've tidied my room."

"Look on the bright side – it shouldn't take you long."

"You haven't seen my room! I could be there for a million years! Parents!" fumed Perce. "Why can't they be straightforward for once?"

Perce and Andy were standing in a quiet corner of the crowded playground. It was the usual hubbub of screaming kids. Footballs were being kicked perilously close to windows, "famous player" stickers were being swapped and skipping-ropes were cutting the air with whiplash ferocity. First years were being dropped off by protective parents. Scarves were adjusted, brightly coloured plastic lunch boxes handed over and noses wiped.

"You will be good, won't you?" one mum whispered as she planted a kiss on a squirming youngster's cheek. Perce glided past, grimaced and hissed, "What she's really saying is: 'You'd better behave or else you're in BIG trouble!'" Andy nodded in agreement.

"Another thing about adults is that they never believe anything you say," continued Perce. "Remember when we told them about Dusa?"

Andy considered this. "Latimer believed us."

"Only 'cos he was potty about Greek myths."

Andy grinned. "*Was*. He's not any more!"

This was true. The deputy head had been

one of the chief sufferers when Ms Dusa, the supply teacher from hell, had mounted her reign of terror. From being his favourite subject, Greek myths had gone right to the top of Mr Latimer's list of Things-We-Don't-Talk-About.

The school bell pierced through the shrieks and screams of the yard. Crowds of children breathed sighs of relief and surged away from their parents towards the sanctuary of the school.

It was then that the man appeared.

Andy saw him first. He gaped. "Look at the size of him!"

Perce whistled softly. "Built like a block of flats."

The man's jacket looked as if someone had taken a doggie-coat off a dachshund and put it on a Rottweiler. Every time he moved, it looked about to split along the seams, and when he swung his arms, unseen muscles rippled inside it like armies of exploring mice.

Perce and Andy stared open-mouthed. Other kids also stood still as the man strode towards them. Then they quickly parted. Moses-like, the man moved through them. Dozens of eyes followed him as he continued across the yard, until he disappeared round the side of the school, going towards the kitchen. There was a pause; a collective letting-out of breath, then normality returned and kids scooted off to another action-packed, fun-filled day of education.

Wonder who he is . . .? mused Andy. He didn't have time to wonder for too long.

"You TWO!"

A loud yell made Perce and Andy turn. Perce groaned. It was Mr Grimes, the school caretaker – "Slimey Grimey". She didn't like him much, but she never let him suspect the fact.

Perce was clever enough to know that care-takers are the real bosses in any school. Everyone knew which teachers Slimey didn't like. Their rooms were never dusted, their bins were never emptied and their radiators were turned off in winter and on in summer. Slimey could make teachers' lives hell. Every Christmas, they would come scurrying to him bearing gifts – usually bottles of whisky – in order to make sure that their year would be trouble free. Sometimes it worked.

"You two, what's that there?"

Andy and Perce followed Slimey's outstretched finger to a piece of paper fluttering about the yard. Andy got on his hands and knees and stared hard at the offending article.

"Eureka!" He straightened and smiled innocently at Slimey. "I believe it is a piece of paper."

Mr Grimes looked as if he would burst. "I *know* it's a piece of paper," he snapped. "Pick it up!"

There it was again! Why couldn't adults say what they meant? Perce was too furious to be careful.

"Go break your leg," she muttered.

"I heard that!" Mr Grimes glared. "Right, for that cheek, you can pick up every bit of litter in the yard. Collect it in a bin and then report back to me so I can make sure you've done it."

Andy began to walk away. "Unlucky, Perce," he laughed.

"Both of you," yelled Slimey. Andy's smile vanished.

"That was your stupid fault," moaned Perce, as Mr Grimes stomped towards his room. "Eureka! Who do you think you are, Aristotle?"

"Me!" exclaimed Andy. "What about you? 'Go break your leg!' Why did you say that?"

Several other stragglers from their class had gathered to snigger at Perce and Andy's plight.

"Actually, Perce, I think you'll find it was Archimedes who said Eureka," said Eddie Johnson.

"Actually, Eddie, I think you'll find my fist

up your nose if you don't shut up!" replied Perce menacingly. Eddie backed away.

"Shall I tell Millsey that you're going to be late?" asked Syreeta.

"Please. Tell her thanks to bozo-brain here," Perce nodded at Andy, "Slimey's got us doing his work for him. She'll understand."

"It wasn't just my fault," muttered Andy defensively.

Well'ard Wally snorted. "It's a good way of getting out of lessons."

"You're never *in* lessons," Perce pointed out.

Well'ard, like Grimes, wasn't the sort to cross or make comments about. He could be considered a trainee caretaker.

"Oh yeah? Well, don't forget to pick these up!" Chuckling, Well'ard helpfully began to empty the contents of his trouser pockets on to the playground.

Perce groaned. "Thanks a bunch, Well'ard, you're all heart!"

★

It took the two of them nearly fifteen minutes to chase the wind-driven litter across the yard, capture it and cage it in the rubbish bin.

They carried the bin round the corner by the kitchen door, and stood playing "You-go-first-why-me-why-not-you" at the top of the cellar steps. Perce was about to upend the bin over Andy's head when they were both shocked rigid by an almighty crashing noise from behind the cellar door.

Perce's head snapped round. "What was that?"

"Slimey must've kicked the bucket."

Ignoring Andy, Perce pelted down the steps. She couldn't see through the frosted-glass panes, but a muffled moaning noise was coming from within.

Andy arrived at her shoulder. "Should we . . . ?"

Perce knocked quietly. "Mr Grimes?" She knocked harder. "Mr Grimes, are you there?" She tried the doorknob and pushed against the door.

WHOOSH!

A searing, scorching blast of hot air made Perce and Andy turn their faces and shield their eyes. It seemed to last for an age. When finally they looked in the room, they were confused and disorientated.

The usually tidy maintenance store was now a disorderly, ramshackle mess. Buckets, mops, toilet paper, towels, bottles, canisters and tables were strewn everywhere. Metal shelving was half ripped off the wall and swung erratically. A filing cabinet lay tipped over on its side.

Lying on the floor among the mess was Mr Grimes. He was clutching his leg and moaning. "Horns . . . it was the horns . . . horns . . ."

Andy gave a groan. "Ooer! Look at that!"

He pointed downwards and covered his mouth to stop himself being sick.

Mr Grimes' left leg was bent at an angle that legs were not designed to be bent at.

"Horns, awful horns and fire . . ."

Perce pushed Andy through the door.

"Quickly, get help!" she ordered. He scrambled up the steps. Perce turned back to the luckless caretaker. She bit her lip.

"Go break your leg," she had told Mr Grimes.

He had.

Chapter Two
The Caretaker Caretaker

". . . AND SO I'M sorry to have to tell you," the Head announced in assembly the following day, "that Mr Grimes will not be returning to the school for some time."

The children listened quietly. Everyone had been shocked by the accident. Slimey hadn't been exactly popular, but he was a familiar figure. Something bad had happened to him in a way that the teachers didn't want to talk about. The pupils sat in uneasy silence, with none of the whispers and bottom-shuffling of a normal assembly.

The Head cleared her throat nervously. She wasn't used to getting the school's undivided attention. "However," she went on, "the news isn't all bad. We've been very fortunate in finding a temporary replacement . . . a sort of caretaker caretaker if you like . . ." The Head tittered nervously at her feeble joke; her audience looked blank. "Anyway, I'd like to introduce you to him . . . him to you . . . er, you to each other . . . right away. Would you all say good-morning, please, to Mr O'Taur."

The Head waved an arm vaguely to indicate someone at the back. Perce and Andy, along with everyone else, craned their necks round. Whispering broke out.

"Where did he spring from?" Andy hissed in Perce's ear. "He wasn't there when we came in, we'd've noticed. He must've . . . flippin' 'eck!"

The whispers cut off suddenly as Mr O'Taur stood up; "unfolded" was how Perce put it to herself. There were a few gasps. Perce stared open-mouthed. "It's that bloke," she hissed at Andy. "The one in the yard, yesterday!"

The new caretaker was built on a monstrous scale. Out of his open-necked sports shirt sprouted a tree-trunk of a neck. His head was in proportion with the rest of him. He had a solid jaw and a wide mouth; his eyes were small and hidden in the fold between high cheek-bones and a low forehead, on which sat eyebrows like giant hairy caterpillars. His hair was a mass of jet-black curls. But the most unusual feature was his nose. It was large and flattish, and wouldn't have been particularly noticeable except for the fact that he had a nose-ring in it.

Funny, thought Perce, caretakers aren't supposed to be trendy!

A voice from deep inside Mr O'Taur rumbled, "Good-morning."

The school's answering "Good-morning" was a shambles. The awkward silence that followed was ended only by the Head's hurried dismissal.

Perce's mind was racing. For some reason that had nothing to do with his size, she didn't like the look of the new caretaker. What had he been doing at the school yesterday, before ... she gave the big man a hard stare ... before Slimey had his accident?

Mr O'Taur left as the first years filed out. Perce turned to Andy and raised her eyebrows. Andy licked his lips and tried to look unconcerned.

"Looks a bit of a bully to me," he said.

"Witch!"

Well'ard Wally's voice grated in Perce's ear. She swung round to glare at him.

"Who is?"

"You are." Miss Mills was busy in the stock cupboard, so Well'ard had stopped even pretending to work. He raised his voice. "Oi! You lot! Perce is a witch!"

17

"How d'you reckon that?" demanded Andy.

Well'ard grinned. "When Slimey made you pick up that paper, Perce said 'Go break your leg', and he did, so that proves it."

Eddie Johnson looked dubious. "No, it doesn't. Witches have pointy hats and black cats and broomsticks and they dance around in convents."

"*Covens*," said Pete. "Convents is nuns."

"Well, they dance anyway."

"I heard they dance around wi' no clothes on," leered Well'ard. "D'you dance around in the nuddy, Perce?"

Perce gave Well'ard one of her best laser mega-death looks. He just grinned at her. Well'ard hadn't got to be the school hard case by worrying about looks from Perce.

"Hey, what if Perce *is* a witch?" Eddie's imagination was getting into top gear. "We could have her in a tent at the school fair . . ."

"Madame Priscilla, Fortune-teller," agreed

Syreeta. Perce winced. She hated it when people used her full name.

Others joined in. "With a tea-towel round her bonce."

"Reading palms."

"And tea-leaves."

"What're tea-leaves?" asked somebody whose tea came in bags.

"And looking into her crystal ball."

"Is there anybody therrrrre?" moaned Well'ard with his eyes shut.

"Yes, there is." Miss Mills appeared in the doorway, having finally tracked down the school's only working staple gun. "What's all this noise about?"

"It's Andy, miss." Well'ard ignored Andy's protests. "He says Perce is a witch."

Miss Mills snorted. "Superstitious nonsense! There are no such things as witches. They're just a myth." Perce jumped as if she'd been shot. "Now, get on with your work."

For the rest of the morning, every time Miss Mills's attention was elsewhere, Well'ard would start chanting, "Witch ... witch ... witch," just loud enough for Perce to hear, but he needn't have bothered. Perce wasn't listening. A small but persistent thought was tugging at the coat-sleeve of her mind and she didn't get much work done for the rest of the day.

"Where are we going?" Andy had to run to keep up with Perce as she charged down the corridor after school.

"To see Mr Latimer."

"What?" Andy stopped dead and goggled at her. "Well, if that's your idea of a fun time ..."

"You needn't come." Perce hadn't even slowed down.

Sighing, Andy followed.

They found Mr Latimer trying to get the computer trolley up the step into his class-room. He didn't look too pleased to see them.

"Could we see you, sir?"

"You *are* seeing me."

This wasn't exactly encouraging, but Perce pressed on. "We wanted to ask you something."

"What's all this 'we'?" muttered Andy, and got a sharp nudge from Perce's elbow.

"Well, what is it?" Mr Latimer lifted the trolley over the step. A castor fell off.

"It's about myths, sir. You know, Greek myths."

Mr Latimer glowered. "That's not a subject I wish to be reminded of, Priscilla."

"But, sir . . ."

"School is over. This is my free time, and I'd rather not spend it discussing unpleasant topics, so if you don't mind . . ."

"But, sir . . ."

". . . or even if you do." Mr Latimer dragged the trolley into his room with a clatter, and closed the door in a very marked manner. Perce seethed.

"Silly old fool, I hope he breaks his —"

"Don't say it!" Andy looked alarmed.

Perce glared at him in disgust. "Not you, too."

Andy gave a sheepish grin.

"Come on."

Again, Andy had to trot to keep up. "Where are we going now?"

"The hospital."

"Hospital? I don't want to go to the hospital."

Perce clenched her fist. "You have a choice. You can go as a visitor or as a patient . . ."

"I know, let's go to the hospital."

"Hello, Mr Grimes."

The face on the pillow didn't look much like Slimey's; it was older and thinner than Perce remembered. For a moment, Mr Grimes looked at them without recognition. Then he said, "Oh . . . it's Perce, isn't it? And Arthur . . ."

"Andy. We brought you these." Andy held out a bunch of flowers, quietly harvested from the local park on their way to the hospital. He started feeling stupid, because there wasn't a vase or anything to put them in.

Mr Grimes forced a smile. "Ta." He waved a hand about. "Just leave them on the table here, one of the nurses will see to them later."

Andy laid down their limp offering, and Perce sat on the hard chair by the bed, glancing round nervously. She hated hospitals.

"Er . . . how are you?"

"Oh, mustn't grumble." Mr Grimes' left leg, smothered in plaster, was held up off the bed by a complicated system of slings.

"Does it hurt?" asked Andy. Perce glared at him.

"Only when I'm awake."

There was an awkward silence.

"Well, it's nice of you to visit me," said Mr Grimes. "I haven't had many visitors . . ."

"Mr Grimes," blurted Perce, leaning forward anxiously, "when we found you, after the accident, you were muttering something . . ."

The pain in Mr Grimes' eyes mingled with a look of astonishment.

"Was I?"

Perce took the plunge. "You were saying something about . . . horns."

Mr Grimes frowned. "Horns? I . . ." His eyes widened and he stared at Perce. "Yes, I remember . . . it must have been the shock, I suppose. Hallucinations. Just for a moment, down there in the cellar, I could've sworn I saw this huge figure, like a man . . . but . . ."

Perce bit her lip. "Yes?"

"But with bull's horns."

A twinge of pain made Mr Grimes close his eyes. When he opened them again, the chair by the bed was empty. The ward doors swung wildly to and fro.

Perce and Andy had gone.

Chapter Three
Myth Illogical

"SO, WHAT ARE you trying to say to me?"

Perce hadn't said a word on the way back from the hospital. Now, in the school yard next morning, she was in a foul humour and Andy couldn't get any sense out of her.

"I'm saying there's something dead weird going on," said Perce darkly. "Slimey said he saw a monster with bull's horns."

"Oh, come on!" scoffed Andy. "He nips in the cellar, and this mad bull leaps on him and breaks his leg. I don't think so."

Perce wasn't used to this sort of opposition from Andy. "Listen, jelly-brain, why would he say he saw horns if he didn't?"

"It was probably a shadow."

"A *what*?"

Andy and Perce joined the pushing, shoving line of their classmates heading for the door.

"You know, like you get in horror films, where someone's all alone in some dark creepy place and the music goes dah-dah-DAH-DAH! and they turn round and there's a huge shadow on the wall of this 'orrible sabre-tooth wotsit about to tear their throat out, and they go 'Aaaaargh!' Then it comes out of the light and it's really a fluffy kitten."

Several people were now staring at Andy. He shrugged.

"Or he might've been delirious."

Perce snorted. "You've got a nerve calling anyone else delirious after all that rubbish about fluffy sabre-tooth kittens."

"Well, I reckon if I'd just had my leg broken in umpteen places, I'd be deliri – wow!"

Perce and Andy gawped open-mouthed. All down the corridor, kids were staring in disbelief.

The school *gleamed*.

The grimy plaster and dull woodwork were suddenly bright and fresh. Windows sparkled, the wood-block floor shone, there wasn't a sweet wrapper, a lump of fluff or even a speck of dust anywhere.

It was the same in their classroom. Miss Mills was wandering round in a daze trying to find things, but it wasn't as if anything was lost or out of place. She just didn't recognize the shining globe, the spotless water pots or the neat felt-tips as the battered, sticky, dusty objects she had put away the night before. Even the computer keyboard, blackened from constant use by thousands of grubby fingers, gleamed as if fresh out of its box. You could even read the letters now, which, as Perce later pointed out, took half the fun out of it.

Andy still looked like a startled goldfish. "Look at this lot! It must have taken him all night!"

Perce stared at him. "*All night?* He couldn't have done it if he'd worked all *week,* not if he was Superman. Some of that dirt was older than me. Some of it was older than *Latimer!*"

There was one new addition to the room. Slap in the middle of the notice-board was a poster on yellow paper with bold, black lettering:

Coming soon!

School Gymnastics Club

In the School Hall
Tuesdays and Thursdays 4–6 pm

Get fit, not fat

Leader: Mr E O'Taur

Perce studied the poster for some time, considering. She muttered "O'Taur" under her breath a few times. Then she turned to Andy. "We're going to the library first lesson, right?"

Andy checked the class timetable on the wall. "Right."

"Good. There's something I want to check."

In the library, Perce made a bee-line for one of the shelves. Without a moment's hesitation, she picked out a book. Andy, curious, read the title: *Myths of Ancient Greece*.

Perce riffled through the book until she found the page she was looking for. She read a section with great concentration, occasionally nodding to herself. Andy was baffled.

Eventually, Perce turned to Andy with a fixed, determined look and held the book open under his nose. Andy shrugged, spread the book out flat, and started to read:

The Legend of the Minotaur

Minos, a strong and cruel king, ruled the island of Crete. He forced King Aegeus of Athens to send him a tribute of seven young men and seven young women of Athens. Their fate was to be sacrificed to a dreadful monster, which lived in the great Labyrinth below Minos's palace at Knossos. This monster had the body of a man, but the head of a bull. It was called the Minotaur . . .

Andy turned to Perce. She was staring at the picture on the opposite page. It showed the Minotaur, a huge and horrifying creature with knotted muscles, a thick neck and a mane of jet-black hair.

"So?"

Perce stared at him. Then she started to explain very slowly and carefully, as though speaking to a very small child: "Because it's about the Minotaur." She paused.

"Mine-otaur." She waited for Andy to catch on. He looked blank. "Mister. Mine. O'Taur."

Andy's eyes bulged as the penny dropped. Then, to Perce's amazement, he started to giggle.

"Oh, leave it out, Perce. You're bein' illogical." Andy paused momentarily, before breaking into a huge grin. "In fact, you're being *myth*illogical – myth illogical. Geddit?"

From this point on, the conversation became rather strained.

Andy pointed out that Perce wouldn't expect to see Hercules nipping down to the Taj Mahal take-away for a chicken vindaloo, would she? She wouldn't find the Wooden Horse of Troy holding up traffic outside Tesco's. Even a thicko like Perce ought to see that things like that didn't happen.

Perce retorted that O'Taur had appeared on the same day that Slimey had had his accident. Perhaps Andy could explain *that* if he was so clever. And while he was about it, could Andy

(World's Number One Genius – NOT!) explain the blast of heat when he and Perce had opened the cellar door?

The World's Number One Genius replied that all the evidence indicated that Perce was stark raving mad; in reply to which Perce invited the World's Number One Genius to step outside and say that again, and offered to telephone for an ambulance and a couple of bottles of blood.

The World's Number One Genius told her to get knotted.

"Anyway," boiled Perce, "what about his name?"

Andy sneered. "Coincidence. I bet there's lots of O'Taurs. It's probably the second most common Irish name after O'Toole or something."

Perce seethed. "And he's got a nose-ring! That's what bulls have."

"So do people," Andy snapped back. "Anyway, that's nothing. My uncle Simon's got

32

a safety-pin through his nose . . . and through both ears."

Perce grabbed Andy by the shoulder and shoved his face towards the book. "Look at the picture. Doesn't it remind you of anyone?"

Andy squinted. "Not really. The bloke in this picture's got horns, for a kick-off."

"Yeah, well . . ." Perce bit her lip. She hadn't worked that point out herself yet.

"He couldn't hide them. I mean, either he's got horns or he hasn't . . ."

"All right, Einstein. We'll see. We're going to keep an eye on Mr O'Taur and find out what he's up to –"

"Who's this 'we'?"

"– and we can start at the gym club tonight."

Chapter Four
Mystery O'Taur

"I'M NOT GOING! I don't see why I should go just because you want to go!"

Perce and Andy were still arguing as they stood in the dinner queue.

"I don't *want* to go," Perce pointed out acidly. "But we've *got* to go to keep an eye on him."

"There you go with this 'we' stuff again," Andy complained. "I don't want to keep an eye on him. I'm not the nutso who thinks the bloke who empties the waste-paper bins is a bull in a boiler suit. Sausage roll and chips, please," he added as he reached the service hatch.

"You don't want chips." Perce shoved Andy to one side. "He doesn't want chips."

"Yes, I do!" protested Andy.

"No, you don't. You've got to lose weight for the gym club."

Perce selected a salad for herself and steered a mutinous Andy to an empty table, where, much to her disgust, Well'ard and Eddie Johnson joined them a few seconds later.

"You two joinin' the gym club, then?" asked Eddie through a mouthful of chips.

"No!" said Andy, eyeing Eddie's chips ravenously.

"Yes!" Perce kicked him under the table. "Both of us."

"What? Andy's doin' gym club?" Well'ard did a bad imitation of a faint and knocked over Perce's orange juice. "Andy gets hot flushes taking the top off his Biro. Every time he sharpens his pencil, he needs a lie-down after."

Andy went into a sulk.

"Well'ard's comin' too," said Eddie.

Perce stopped mopping juice. "Get out of town!"

Well'ard did a muscle-man pose. "Thought I'd show you how it's done."

"You must be joking." Perce stared at Well'ard. "You've never done PE in your life. You always bring a note."

"Yeah, well, that's a matter of principle, gettin' out of PE," explained Well'ard. "But keep fit's different. You've got to be fit to get in the SAS."

Perce groaned. Well'ard had told everyone in the class at least fifty times that he was going to join the SAS.

Well'ard continued to explain his momentous decision. "Anyway, that new bloke looks like he knows how to get people fit. Couple of weeks with him, even Andy might be able to bend a stick of liquorice." Well'ard pushed his plate away and wandered off, nudging people to make them spill their food as he went.

"What's SAS stand for, anyway?" asked Eddie, finishing his last chip.

"Stupid And Sad," muttered Perce, glaring after Well'ard.

Even before the gym club started, it was clear that, as far as the staff were concerned, Mr O'Taur could do no wrong. Teachers who, in Perce's view, ought to have been kept in cages purred like pussy cats whenever the caretaker was around. There was hardly any litter. A discarded crisp packet stood out like a giraffe on an iceberg.

Everything was so clean and ran so well that few people noticed – or cared – that the new caretaker was very rarely about. Grimey had always been pottering around the school, but Mr O'Taur only seemed to put in an appearance when there was a particular job to be done. Occasionally he was glimpsed going down the steps to his store in the old cellar, but apart from that nobody seemed to be bothered about where he spent most of his time. Nobody, that is, except Perce.

"I don't know what he does in there!" Andy snapped in exasperation. "If he wants to sit in the cellar all day, that's up to him. Maybe he's making a sailing ship out of paper-clips or something."

"You wait," said Perce grimly. "He's up to something."

"Why should he be up to anything?"

"Because he's the Minotaur!"

"You keep saying that," complained Andy, "but he's not doing anything except keeping the school clean. What makes you so sure?"

"Well, there's his name, for a start . . ."

"Oh, his *name*," sneered Andy. "Yes, his last name, we've heard about that. What about his first name?"

Perce scowled. This was another weak spot in her argument, and she knew it.

"His first name starts with an E." Andy pressed home his advantage. "It's on all the gym club posters. What d'you reckon it stands for? The Eric O'Taur? The Eddie O'Taur? The Ernest O'Taur? Or maybe, the Egbert-no-bacon O'Taur?" Perce chewed her lip and said nothing. "Come on, Perce, let's forget the gym club . . ."

"We are going," said Perce, twisting Andy's arm, "to the gym club."

"Get off, that hurts." Andy rubbed his arm and said bitterly, "You haven't got any arguments. You're just in a bad mood because you think I might be right."

To that, Perce said nothing. Mostly because it was true.

The gym club was a lot better than Perce and Andy had expected. There was a good turnout. Eddie was there in fluorescent-pink cycling shorts and so was Well'ard in his dad's old rugby bags and last year's trainers. About thirty other kids turned up.

Mr O'Taur was professionally kitted out in an expensive-looking track suit. He was very business-like; he just explained what he wanted the group to do, clapped his hands once, and let them get on. He never wasted words, and he never raised his voice. He never needed to.

One reason for this was that nobody felt like cheeking someone who looked quite capable of tearing pianos apart with his bare hands, and another was that the exercises were fun. There were sit-ups and stretching exercises and push-ups, all the usual things; nevertheless Mr O'Taur managed to turn everything into a game – a game where everyone felt they'd won. He would always change the activity before anyone got bored or tired out; he never forced anyone to do anything. He never praised anyone, but he never criticized either. Perce and Andy finished the first session feeling fresher than when they'd started.

"It's not right," Perce muttered darkly, "I should feel knackered, but I don't."

Andy sniffed. "You're just looking for something to moan about. That was brill!"

In the following sessions the exercises became more complicated and tougher, but even unsporty types like Eddie started to feel fitter and more confident, and proud of their new skills.

Perce began to feel less sure of herself. Maybe she had made a mistake about Mr O'Taur. It still seemed wrong to Perce that she suddenly found herself doing the sort of gymnastics she'd never have dreamt of being able to do – the sort you should only be able to do if you weighed three stone and came from Romania. But she was doing them, and so were Andy, Well'ard, Eddie and all the others, and it felt good, so what was she worrying about? Maybe Andy was right after all.

Then, three things happened.

The first was a delivery. A van pulled up at the front entrance during morning break. Curious kids watched as two sweating delivery men and Mr O'Taur manoeuvred a large, heavy object wrapped in layers of bubble film into the school. By lunch-time, the school's new acquisition had been unpacked, and Perce and Andy watched as Mr O'Taur strolled round it, lovingly stroking the leather hide. It stood in the middle of the hall, its four splayed wooden legs giving it a slightly comic air that was also, at least to Perce, a little disturbing. It was a huge vaulting-horse.

The second thing happened a few minutes later. Mr O'Taur spotted Perce hanging around and gave her the delivery-note that had come with the horse to take to the school secretary. Half-way down the corridor, Perce stopped so suddenly that Andy, who had been following, bumped into her. She was staring at the note. Without a word, she shoved it under

Andy's nose.

Andy examined the note, and then looked enquiringly at Perce.

"Look at the signature!"

Mr O'Taur had signed to say that he had received the delivery. There was his name in his neat, surprisingly small handwriting: Emmanuel O'Taur.

Andy still didn't get it.

"Emmanuel," Perce explained slowly, her voice shaking with suppressed excitement. "Not Eric, or Eddie, or Ernest: Emmanuel. If you're called Emmanuel, d'you know what people call you for short?"

Andy shook his head. He didn't know anyone called Emmanuel.

"They call you Manny," said Perce, rolling the word round her tongue. "Manny. Manny O'Taur."

The third thing happened a couple of days later. Nobody saw it happen, and for some time, nobody even knew that it had.

It started with an argument. Pete said that the gym club had been cancelled because of a parents' evening. Syreeta said the Head had decided that the gym club could go ahead as usual. They were still arguing as the bell went, so Pete said they should go and ask Mr O'Taur. He would probably be in the store, and if they hurried they wouldn't be too late for registration.

Nobody saw them go down the cellar steps and hesitate in front of the green door.

"Mr O'Taur?" called Syreeta.

The cellar door swung open. A rumbling sound came from inside. It might have been a very deep voice saying, "Come in."

Syreeta hung back, but Pete gave her a scornful look and stepped through the doorway, so then, of course, Syreeta had to go in too.

The cellar door swung closed behind them.

Chapter Five
It's Your Vault

THERE *WAS* A gym club that night — a special one. When the kids walked into the gym, there in the middle was the new vaulting-horse. Mr O'Taur stood next to it, patting and stroking the leather top.

"It looks just like an animal," whispered Perce to Andy. "All that leather, just like a —"

"Don't tell me . . ." Andy shook his head. "Let me guess. You're going to say 'like a bull'. You're right, it does — apart from the horns . . .

and the tail . . . and the face . . . and the . . . ow!"
Perce stared hard at Andy. Andy rubbed his
shoulder. "I wish you'd stop doing that," he
grimaced.

"Don't be sarky, then."

"Sit down!" Their squabbling was interrupted by Mr O'Taur's deep voice.

The kids immediately settled down and
listened attentively as Mr O'Taur began to
explain how to vault. "Run fast at the horse,
bounce on the springboard, keep your legs
wide apart, place your hands in the middle of
the horse and vault over it to land on the other
side." The instructions were delivered in a
matter-of-fact voice and a this-is-so-simple-
you-can-all-do-it manner. "When you have
mastered this, we will progress to more complicated and *interesting* leaps and vaults."

"What's he mean by interesting?" hissed
Perce. As if in answer to her seemingly
unheard question, Mr O'Taur suddenly sprinted at the horse, launched himself at the front

end and soared upwards. As he floated in mid-air, he twisted and flipped his body round once . . . twice . . . three times. This sent him spinning over the horse in a perfect arc. His spiralling descent and two-footed landing were achieved with a grace and an ease that seemed unnatural

There was silence. The kids stared, aghast. Even Perce was impressed: Mr O'Taur hadn't even bothered to use the springboard.

"I don't expect you to do that straight away," Mr O'Taur smiled. The kids chuckled at the joke. "It is an example of what you can do with practice. Years and years of it," he added. "Now, get into line."

The next hour was filled with hurtling bodies and loud cheers and applause as kids leaped, sprang and vaulted over the horse as best they could. The whole gym was buzzing with a concentrated excitement. Despite herself, Perce was lost in the thrill of defeating gravity for a split second.

Even Eddie Johnson's unfortunate mishap couldn't dampen the enthusiasm for vaulting. It happened on his third vault: he ran hard at the springboard, jumped on to it and bounced over the front of the horse, legs splayed. Unfortunately he forgot to put his hands down, in order to leapfrog the horse, and he landed, legs wide apart, in the middle of the hard leather top.

THUMP!

Eddie's lips pursed and both his pupils shot towards his nose. A pleading, squeaking sound came from somewhere deep inside as he fought for breath.

It was one of those incidents that would normally have had everyone laughing like hyenas, but no one did: except for Well'ard, who laughed at everything.

"I bet he can sing soprano now!" he chortled. "I reckon he's going to be well bruised on his —"

"Silence!" ordered Mr O'Taur. Well'ard kept

48

his mouth shut. Mr O'Taur turned to Eddie. "Hard luck, lad, try again."

A week or two ago, Eddie would have howled and gone home. Today, he staggered cross-legged to the back of the line, ready for another attempt.

The vaulting continued.

Towards the end of the session, as they stood waiting their turn, Andy turned to Perce. "Shame that Syreeta and Pete missed this today. They'd have enjoyed it."

"Yeah," nodded Perce.

"Wonder what's wrong with them?"

"They're skivin'," said Well'ard, who'd been earwigging the conversation.

"How do you know that?" asked Perce.

"I saw them this morning," said Well'ard. "I told Millsey I'd seen them and I reckoned that they were skivin', but she didn't believe me."

"I wonder why?" Perce's sarcasm was hardly subtle.

Well'ard returned her stare. "You sayin' I tell lies?"

"Well'ard," replied Perce, "if they gave medals for lying, you'd win the Olympic gold."

Well'ard huffed a snort of hurt disapproval and put on his world-famous wounded puppy look. Perce felt a twinge of conscience. Maybe Well'ard *was* telling the truth. Also, she was curious to know about Pete and Syreeta. Against her better judgement she decided to give Well'ard the benefit of the doubt.

"All right, Well'ard, where did you see them? If you saw them at all," she added for her own protection.

Well'ard turned from his position at the front of the line of vaulters. He gave Perce a told-you-so look before replying. "They were in the yard near Mr O'Taur's office." He turned to face the vaulting-horse. "GERANIUM!"

"Geronimo," corrected Eddie in a strangled voice. His eyes were still watering.

"Yeah, him an' all," replied Well'ard as he sprinted for the horse, arms and legs flaying the air.

"Nice style," commented Andy. "Dead elegant."

"More like a dead elephant," mused Lee.

Perce ignored them. "Near Mr O'Taur's office . . .?" she murmured.

"Come on, Perce!" She was interrupted by Andy nudging her. "It's your turn." She looked over to the horse where Mr O'Taur stood waiting. He was beckoning towards her.

"Oh . . . er . . . you go next, Andy. I think I've just pulled a muscle."

"By standing still?" Andy shrugged his shoulders and began sprinting towards the waiting horse.

Perce didn't have to vault again. After Andy had completed his vault, Mr O'Taur clapped his hands. "That's it. Stretching-out exercises."

As the kids began stretching their legs and arms Mr O'Taur walked among them, checking that they were warming down properly.

"Good," he said. "Now, listen carefully." He touched several of the kids on the head. "Robert Williams, Justin Green, Nitesh Patel, Sam Skinner, Oliver Moore and Delroy Peters. You have all worked very well tonight and show a lot of potential."The named kids began to glow with pride. "As a reward you can stay and help me put away the vaulting-horse."

There were groans, but not from the six "volunteers" – they were honoured at being chosen. It was the rest of the group who were disappointed. Everyone except Perce. Normally she would have moaned about how sexist it was that only boys had been asked to put something heavy away, but tonight she wanted to get out of the gym as quickly as possible.

"The rest of you," thundered Mr O'Taur, "off you go."

Perce was the first out of the door.

Chapter Six
Absent Friends . . .

THE ALARM BELLS in Perce's head were ringing full blast next day. Pete and Syreeta were still away. Perce had waited anxiously for them in the yard before registration, but they hadn't appeared. Miss Mills asked if anyone knew anything about their absence when she took the register.

"They're skivin' again!" Well'ard shouted out, but Miss Mills waved him away with a dismissive, "Yes, thank *you*, Walter." Well'ard sat back in his chair and folded his arms grumpily.

"Now, sit still, everyone, while I get some paper."

As Miss Mills headed to the stock cupboard, Perce turned to Andy. "They're away again."

"So?"

"So, it's obvious, isn't it?"

"Yeah, it's obvious that they're ill," Andy said sarcastically. "For instance, they may have broken their legs, got a cold —"

"But, Andy —"

"— caught mumps —"

"Andy —"

"— got bumps —"

"Andy —"

"— suffered lumps." Andy was now in full rhyming mode.

"ANDY!" screamed Perce. "What if O'Taur has done something to Pete and Syreeta!"

"Priscilla! Why are you shouting?" Miss Mills stormed back into the room. Perce didn't have time to respond. "And why haven't you started to collect the registers? It's your turn, hurry up."

Perce stared at Andy; he smirked back. Going round all the classrooms to collect the registers and the lists of people who were absent was supposed to be an honour, but Perce found it a chore. She headed off towards Mr Latimer's classroom with Miss Mills's register and absence list. On it were Pete and Syreeta's names. Perce shook her head and began worrying again.

Twenty minutes later, Perce stood outside the school secretary's office. Not bad, she thought, if you've got to do a boring job, then waste as much time as possible doing it.

"Won't be a minute," called Mrs Robbins, the secretary.

"Take as long as you want," mumbled Perce. As she stood waiting, she flicked through the absence lists.

Pete and Syreeta from Perce's class.

Robert Williams from Mr Latimer's class.

Justin Green from Ms Paine's.

None from Mrs "What-a-Dragon" Needit's class. No one would dare be away, thought Perce.

Mr White's class – Nitesh Patel and Sam Skinner. Perce stopped flicking – where had she recently heard those names?

Oliver Moore from Mrs Jones's . . .

Perce went very cold. She glanced quickly through the other lists . . . and found what she was half expecting and half hoping she wouldn't. Absent from Miss Smith's class – Delroy Peters.

"*Everyone* Mr O'Taur chose to help put away the vaulting-horse last night is away today!" Perce yelled at Andy at break-time.

"Perce . . ." sighed Andy.

"All six of them are on the absent list."

"Coincidence?" suggested Andy.

"Coincidence!" Perce shouted back at him. "He's *done* something to them; like he's done

56

something to Pete and Syreeta!"

"Oh come off it, Perce, where's your proof?" Andy was fed up with Perce going on about Mr O'Taur.

"The volunteers are away after he asked them to stay behind; Pete and Syreeta were seen near his store-room; his name and . . . and . . ." Perce was running out of steam, "and he's really different and strange!"

"If being strange makes you a mythological monster," Andy snapped back, "then all teachers, my parents, and most adults are mythological monsters — and so are you!"

"Andy . . ."

"You're being stupid. Mythological monsters don't go round being nice and cleaning schools and running gym clubs!"

Although he was tired of hearing Perce's unfounded accusations, there was another reason why Perce's suspicions about Mr O'Taur annoyed Andy. It was one which he would never have thought possible: he was enjoying the gym sessions! The new vaulting-horse was brilliant! And the way that Mr O'Taur coached, persuaded and encouraged everyone was great. Mr O'Taur was rapidly becoming Andy's hero.

"Perce, you're just being paranormal!" Andy began to wave his arms and shake his head around manically. "Watch out! Watch out! The walls are closing in, everybody!"

Perce gave him a look of contempt. "You mean paranoid."

Andy hated it when Perce corrected him. "OK, paranoid," he snarled. "Why don't you go and take a running jump off a parapet?" The air between the two of them was now more than frosty, it was positively Arctic.

"Ha ha," sneered Perce. "Talking of 'para' words, you're going to need a *para*medic in a minute!"

"Oh yeah!" Andy stared straight into Perce's eyes. "I'm fed up with you threatening me all the time. Just 'cos you're a girl you think you can pick on me!" The ferocity of Andy's voice stopped Perce replying.

"I'm sick of you," he continued. "You always think you're right. Always telling me what to do, always telling me what to think. Just because Syreeta and Pete are skiving off school, you have to blame O'Taur, 'cos it fits in with your stupid ideas! Well, I think O'Taur's all right! He's not a monster, he's brilliant! I like *him* and I don't like *you*!"

Perce felt her face beginning to flush and tears welling up in her eyes. She stood stunned under Andy's attack.

"I'm not walking home with you any more. So, forget tomorrow morning: I'll walk to school on my own!" Andy stormed away and headed for the football game taking place in the yard.

Perce stood flabbergasted. Tears began to trickle down her face. She'd never argued like this with Andy before. She fought back further tears and gritted her teeth. She wasn't someone to admit that she was wrong. "All right, I'll prove it to you!" she shouted. She wiped her tears away as some passing first years began to point at her and laugh. Perce realized that she was making a spectacle of herself and needed to regain her composure. She covered her face and ran off, head down, towards the toilets.

If Perce had looked up, as she dashed across the playground, she would have seen Mr O'Taur standing in the corner by the kitchens, surveying the scene. As she ran into the toilets, Mr O'Taur smiled, turned, made his way down the cellar steps and disappeared into his store-room.

At lunch-time, Perce made another visit to the school library. After searching the shelves, she approached the desk and said, "Excuse me, Mrs Jones," in her "please-help-me-as-I'm-totally-useless" voice.

"Yes?" snapped Mrs Jones, clearly thinking that her library would be a nice, quiet, orderly place if only kids wouldn't keep coming in to borrow books.

"I'm looking for the book on Greek myths. I can't find it on the shelf."

"Then it must be out!"

"When is it due back?" enquired Perce sweetly.

"Just a minute." Glowering, Mrs Jones checked the card files. "It's out on a long-term loan," she eventually announced.

"Oh!" Perce was disappointed. "I needed it for a project. Who's got it out?"

Mrs Jones peered at the ticket. Even before she replied, Perce knew what the answer was going to be.

"Mr O'Taur."

Perce's stomach lurched. She mumbled a "thanks" and turned away. Then a thought struck her. She hurried over to the set of encyclopedias and picked out the *Man to Myth* volume.

Sitting at a table, she began to flick through

the pages, looking for "Minotaur". After a few seconds she stopped and stared in horror. She flipped several pages back and forward, but there was no mistake.

The page in the encyclopedia that should have contained the entry on the Minotaur had been ripped out!

Chapter Seven
A Bull by the Horns

"WHAT'S WRONG WITH you?" asked Perce's father.

Ha! thought Perce. What you mean is: "Stop sulking or I'll give you something to sulk about."

"Is something the matter, love?"

Perce looked up. Her mum must have been reading that book on *Good Parenting* again.

"School," she said. That usually cut off further enquiries; parents never wanted to know what happened at school, it was bad enough coping with what happened at home.

"Homework, is it?"

Perce nodded. That was safe. She knew she couldn't tell her mum about Mr O'Taur. "I've got to do a project on a Greek myth, but all the books are out."

Her father grunted. "Why not try the town library?"

Perce inwardly kicked herself. She'd been so upset she hadn't thought of that. Of course! Mr O'Taur could hardly have ripped out every reference to the Minotaur in the main library. She checked the clock.

"I can't go now, it'll be shut."

"What do you have to find out?"

Perce stared. Her dad hadn't offered to help her with homework since she'd presented him with a maths problem that had made him chew his tie and swear in frustration. He'd spent hours wrestling with it. He'd nearly throttled Perce when she moaned at him next day for getting the answer wrong.

"Well . . ." Perce hesitated, ". . . it's about the Minotaur."

"That's the one with Theseus, isn't it?"

Perce gaped. Her dad actually knew something!

"Er, yes . . . well, all I know so far is that the Minotaur lived in a labyrinth. What's a labyrinth?"

"Well, it's a sort of . . . it's like a . . . you get them . . ." her father was clearly already regretting his helpful impulse. Explaining things to Perce always gave him a headache. "It's a sort of maze."

"Like that famous one at Hampton Court — made out of hedges . . .?"

"No. More like tunnels. Underground."

Light dawned. Perce stared at him as the picture of a certain green wooden door with frosted panes of glass sprang into her mind. "You mean, like a cellar?"

★

Perce spent the next day doing some hard thinking. None of her missing schoolmates had returned. Andy was still ignoring her. How could she find out what O'Taur was up to?

The answer came to her at break, when Well'ard asked Perce whether she was going to the gym club that afternoon.

Perce's eyes gleamed. Of course! While the gym club was on, she knew where O'Taur would be. She had to discover what was going on in the cellar, and this was her chance!

After lessons had ended, she went out into the playground, tiptoed up to the gym wall, and peered through the window. Inside, there was a line of children taking it in turns to vault. Andy, Well'ard, Lee, Eddie, they were all there. As usual there was no fuss, no noise, just a studied concentration.

There was a change to the vaulting-horse. It horrified Perce, though she couldn't have said why. Since the last session, Mr O'Taur had fitted what looked like a pair of motorbike handlebars to the front of the horse, so that it looked as if it had grown ... Perce gulped ... horns.

Mr O'Taur issued his commands. Each pupil took it in turns to run at the horse, jump on the springboard and vault; but now, the more adventurous ones were doing handflicks from the handlebar-horns. After each jump, Mr O'Taur would offer criticism tempered with expert advice. Once or twice he even demonstrated a vault himself, using the horns as handgrips and somersaulting over the horse with ease.

Perce turned away. She hadn't been seen and her presence seemed not to have been missed at the club. She began to head across the playground towards the cellar door.

A burst of applause came from the gym. Perce glanced back over her shoulder. Someone must have done a good leap, she thought. At least she knew where O'Taur was.

She crept down the steps to the green wooden door and stood before it, her hand poised over the doorknob. She peered through the frosted panes but could see nothing. This is it, she thought, here goes. Her hand moved downwards and took a firm grip on the brass doorknob.

Perce half expected the door to be locked. If she was being truthful with herself, she was half hoping it *would* be. It wasn't. The doorknob turned. She pushed against the door and it began to glide open. Shaking, she pushed the door fully open and stepped inside.

What Perce expected to see and what she actually saw were very different. Yes, there were metal shelves full of toilet rolls, linen towels and bottles of disinfectant, but they seemed to be blurred. Perce couldn't make out their exact shapes. She blinked, trying to focus on the shelves, and moved forwards.

Suddenly, the cellar seemed to explode in a blast of heat. This was what she had felt when

Mr Grimes had had his accident. From the far side of the store she could hear noises. Deep echoing moans were intermingled with high-pitched yells and screams. Perce froze, her heart pounding.

What was it?

Shaking with fear, Perce moved in further. By now the shelves had disappeared and Perce could make out a faint flickering light in the distance. This was too much! She turned to go back and gasped in horror. Instead of seeing the store-room she saw a long stone tunnel illuminated by flaming torches. She panicked – it wasn't possible! The torches lit up a series of murals on the walls. Bright-red pictures showed bulls with people leaping over them.

Perce turned again, but in every direction she could see only more tunnels leading into the distance. As she spun around she could hear a roaring. She was trapped in a maze. This was a labyrinth! She had been right about O'Taur, but how could that help her now?

Her heart pounded. How was it possible?

Almost fainting with horror, Perce stumbled back a step and flung a hand out to support herself against a tunnel wall. Something sharp and cold dug into her palm.

The shock cleared Perce's head. She was clutching a metal shelf! Something seemed to be tugging her onwards, into the labyrinth. The bulls that adorned the walls seemed to be staring down and mocking her: "You can't escape, you can't escape!" She could only *see* the rough rock walls of the tunnel, but she could *feel* shelves. Whatever her eyes were showing her, her fingers were telling her she was still in the cellar.

Closing her eyes firmly, Perce twisted, turned, tripped, stumbled and groped her way along the shelves, tripping over mops and buckets until at last she found the smooth roundness of the doorknob beneath her fingers. Perce yanked the cellar door open, staggered up the steps, and, with an overwhelming sense of relief, gasped in the safe and welcoming cold air of the playground.

"Where've you been?"

"What's wrong with her?"

Perce looked up. Still dazed, she could make out the shapes of Eddie and Well'ard making their way home from the gym club.

"O'Taur . . . labyrinth . . . bulls . . . proof. . . in there," gibbered Perce, pointing at the cellar. Eddie stared at her in amazement.

"She's been at the wine–gums again," said Well'ard.

"No . . . in there, it's terrible. We've got to get help."

Before they had a chance to protest, Perce dragged them both towards the staffroom. She tried to tell them about O'Taur, and the labyrinth, but she kept getting mixed up and leaving things out. Eddie and Well'ard couldn't make head nor tail of the rambling account Perce tried to give them, but her terror was unmistakably real. By the time they had reached the staffroom, Eddie and Well'ard had got hold of the idea that Pete and Syreeta were trapped in the cellar, and in some sort of danger.

Eddie knocked on the grey staffroom door and they waited for someone to answer.

"There's got to be someone there!" moaned Perce.

"Even if there is, will they believe us?" asked Eddie. Well'ard stared at him and nodded.

"Leave it to me." He then hammered on the door, with his fists, arms and, finally, his feet.

"What on earth are you doing?" The door jerked open. Mr Latimer stood glaring.

"Sir, sir, it's an emergency!" yelled Well'ard, waving his arms about. "We've seen smoke coming from the caretaker's store. It could be on fire!" He turned and winked at Eddie. Perce was impressed with Well'ard's ability to invent stories in a microsecond. Years of practice, she thought.

"Are you sure?" Mr Latimer eyed the three

kids suspiciously. Well'ard was the school's All-Time-Lie-Telling Champion and Eddie had a bigger imagination than Steven Spielberg – but Perce?

"All right," he said, "I'm coming."

They took the short cut through the kitchens, clattered down the steps, and stood before the cellar door.

"There's no sign of smoke." Latimer peered at the door. There was a pause. He glared suspiciously at Perce.

"There's no time to explain, sir," cried Perce. "There's something terrible in there and I can prove it! Look!"

Perce turned the doorknob and flung the cellar door open.

"Good-evening, Mr Latimer. What can I do for you?"

Perce stared in horror. There were no flickering torches, no heat, no noise, no labyrinth; just shelves, buckets, mops and, sitting calmly at his desk, reading a newspaper, Mr O'Taur.

Chapter Eight
Are You Ready, Eddie?

AS THEY PICKED up litter in the yard next day, Well'ard and Eddie complained bitterly that Perce had got them into another fine mess. Perce insisted that it wasn't HER fault.

"Oh, yeah?" sneered Well'ard. "Who was it then who talked us into dragging Latimer down to the caretaker's store with some cock-and-bull story about a Greek monster in a lavvy-plinth —"

"Labyrinth," corrected Perce.

Well'ard scowled. "What is a laby-thingy, anyway?"

"It's an underground maze," Perce explained. "It's where the Minotaur lived."

"Yeah?" Eddie was impressed. "What, like secret passages and stuff?"

"That's right. It was at Knossos –"

"Bless you!"

"I wasn't sneezing, you wally!"

Perce explained that the Labyrinth of Greek mythology was in Crete. King Minos had ordered a giant underground maze to be built beneath his palace. People Minos didn't like got shoved down into the Labyrinth, and they got lost –

"– and wandered around until they died of starvation and turned into skellingtons, right?" Well'ard watched too many Indiana Jones movies.

"Wrong. Until the Minotaur got them."

Eddie and Well'ard shivered.

Andy wandered past. He pretended he hadn't seen Perce.

"Anyway, I reckon that's what happened to Pete and Syreeta and the others. They got into the Labyrinth."

Well'ard scratched his head. "But you said the Labyrinth was in Crossness."

Perce tried again. The Labyrinth was in *Knossos*. Well'ard was still puzzled. Why, he wanted to know, was the Labyrinth in a crate? Perce's head began to ache. No, it wasn't in a crate. Knossos was a place in *Crete*. Crete was an island. In the Mediterranean. The Mediterranean was a *sea*.

Well'ard still wasn't happy. "Yeah, well, what I meantersay is: how can it be there and here as well? Eh, clever-clogs?"

Eddie interrupted to ask why, if Perce had got into the Labyrinth through the cellar, it hadn't been there when they took Latimer to see it.

Perce thought hard. Perhaps, she said, the

Labyrinth wasn't there all the time.

This baffled Well'ard. He didn't understand how something could be there one minute and gone the next. To be honest, neither did Perce.

Eddie had another question. "If there is a Minotaur, what's it doing in our school cellar?"

Perce had an idea about that. "What if Dusa's being here opened some sort of . . . dunno . . . some sort of door, so that other things could come through? I mean, other monsters from the Greek myths? What if O'Taur found that door?"

"So what does he want with Pete and Syreeta?"

Perce's patience ran out. "How am I supposed to know? Perhaps I can find something out in the library. I'm going there after school."

"If we ever get this litter picked up," moaned Eddie.

"Litter!" complained Perce bitterly. "What a waste of time! If we left it, it'd still all be gone by morning. O'Taur would see to that."

"I reckon," said Eddie thoughtfully, "Latimer feels guilty about leaving stuff for O'Taur to clear up, so he gets us to do it."

"But it's O'Taur's *job* to clear up!" complained Well'ard. "That doesn't make sense."

"It's how teachers think," Perce pointed out. "It's not *supposed* to make sense."

This was an unanswerable argument, so nobody answered it. Anyway, just then the bell went for the end of break.

During the dinner hour – while Perce and Andy were working very hard at ignoring each other from opposite ends of the school yard – Well'ard took Eddie to one side.

"Lissen," he said, with a mouth full of bubble gum, "what d'you reckon to this Minotaur lark? You reckon Perce could be right?"

Eddie looked blank. "Well, what if she is?"

"What if *we* found the Labyrinth an' this bull-bloke? We'd be heroes, wouldn't we?"

"Yeah," breathed Eddie. His technicolour imagination was immediately flooded with front-page stories in the paper, TV interviews and victory parades . . .

"What about it, then?"

"I'm in." Eddie's face fell. "Hey, but it's no good."

"What isn't?"

"Well, they won't believe us, will they? All the teachers have got this weird idea that I exaggerate things. And they think you tell lies."

"Me?" asked Well'ard, the picture of injured innocence. "Why?"

"Because you *do* tell lies," said Eddie bluntly. "All the time."

"Only to teachers," protested Well'ard. "That's not tellin' lies, that's misleadin' the enemy."

"It's teachers we've got to convince."

"Huh!" said Well'ard, nettled. "Teachers! Fancy not believin' you, just 'cos you tell lies."

For a while, Eddie thought and Well'ard sulked.

Eventually, Eddie's face lit up. What he and Well'ard needed was a witness to go and find the Labyrinth with them: someone who the teachers would listen to, someone who didn't tell lies.

"Flamin' 'eck," grimaced Well'ard. The thought of someone so depraved they never told lies made him feel quite peculiar. "Where can we find someone like that?"

Eddie suggested Jane Flamstead.

"Biggest liar in the school," said Well'ard glumly. "She told me she saw Elvis Presley fryin' cod at the Ocean Wave Chipperama."

"She never!" Eddie was shocked. "If you can't trust a kid whose dad's a vicar, who can you trust?" He brooded for a moment and then said, "She didn't see him really, I s'pose?"

"Nah." Well'ard was scornful. "I went and looked. Nothin' like him."

Eddie sighed. Then he brightened. "Hey,

what about Claire Greene? She comes to the gym club with her mate."

"Huh! Grassy Greene! She's shopped so many people she ought to be called Sainsbury's."

Eddie agreed, but the point was that the teachers believed everything Claire said. That was exactly the sort of witness they needed. All Well'ard had to do was to get her down to the cellar . . .

"How'm I supposed to do that?" Well'ard protested. "She wouldn't go anywhere with me. She'd think I was goin' to thump her." He considered. "She'd be right an' all."

Eddie looked cunning. "Tell her you saw some fourth years smokin' in there."

"D'you think she'd come then?"

"Is the Pope a Catholic?"

Well'ard's brow furrowed. "I dunno. Is he?"

Eddie rolled his eyes. "Just tell her. Straight after school, OK? I'll see you by the cellar steps."

★

At home-time, Perce made a bee-line for the town library, and was soon poring over a book on Greek Mythology.

In some accounts of the legend, read Perce, *the Minotaur is said to be King Minos's son Asterius, or Asterion. Others say the Minotaur was Minos himself. All the legends agree that the monster lived in the Labyrinth under Minos's palace.*

The people of Athens had lost a war against Minos, so he made them pay him a tribute. Every nine years, seven young men and seven young women were sent to be sacrificed to the Minotaur.

Prince Theseus of Athens offered to be one of the sacrifices . . .

Perce read on and made notes until she reached a passage in the book that made her snap the point off her pencil. Shocked, she carefully re-read the section:

One of the most interesting things about the whole Minotaur legend is the bull dance . . .

As Perce read on, her eyes grew round with horror.

Eddie's plan worked. Nearly.

Well'ard told Claire he'd seen a few of the fourth years sneaking into the cellar with a packet of ciggies, and an avenging gleam appeared in her eye. But she refused to investigate without her friend Stacey.

Well'ard reckoned that was OK. Two witnesses were better than one – that's what Well'ard's brother said and he should know. He was in court often enough.

The first thing they saw when they rounded the corner of the yard was Eddie, dressed in knee-breeches, white stockings, a velvet jacket, a little black hat with Mickey Mouse ears and a red cape draped over his shoulder.

Well'ard's mouth dropped open. "What are you got up as?"

"The local operatic society left it here when they did *Carmen*. Good, isn't it? I'm a matador."

Well'ard glowered. "You look more like a doormat."

Eddie struck a pose. "Zey call me, El Macho."

"You're sure it's not El Plonko?"

Stacey giggled, while Claire eyed Eddie with distrust. "What's he wearing that for?"

"Beautiful *senorita*, I dedicate ze ears of zis bull to you."

Well'ard dragged Eddie to one side. "What are you playin' at?"

"We're going to fight a bull, aren't we? So I'm going to be a bullfighter."

"Well'ard!" Claire hissed. "What about these boys you saw going —"

"Yeah! Right!" Well'ard gave Eddie a poisonous glance, and turned back to the girls. "Yeah, they're in there. I saw 'em. Def'nit'ly." He pointed down the steps to the cellar door.

Stacey shivered. "We ought to go and get a teacher."

"Ah, but then they might sneak out before

you got back," said Eddie hurriedly. "But if you go in now you can see who they are."

Giving Claire no time to think about the holes in that argument, Eddie and Well'ard propelled the girls through the door.

Right until that moment, if they'd been honest, Eddie and Well'ard would have had to admit they'd been expecting to find themselves in the caretaker's store after all. Eddie even had a couple of stories in reserve – one for the girls, and one for Mr O'Taur if he happened to be in there.

Once they were through the door, though, they found themselves in a tunnel of rock. There wasn't a mop or a toilet roll in sight.

Eddie and Well'ard were almost as startled as Stacey and Claire.

"This isn't right." Claire's eyes grew round. "I'm sure it shouldn't be like this –" She broke off as the door slammed shut behind them with a crash that echoed down the tunnel. They were plunged into darkness. Stacey grabbed Claire's arm. Well'ard only just stopped himself from grabbing Eddie's.

"It's the wind," quavered Well'ard. "It must've got up, and blown the door closed."

"The door isn't the only thing that's got the wind up," muttered Eddie.

As the echoes faded, a red glow appeared in the distance.

"There you are, see?" Well'ard pointed. "It's all right. That's probably the boilers."

Nobody looked convinced, but there was no going back, so they went on. After only a few steps, they came to a point where the tunnel split. The red glow seemed to come from both directions.

"Which way now?" asked Claire.

As if in answer, the red glow suddenly burst out of the tunnels like flame. Blasts of hot air blew at them, sending them clawing blindly out of the way. Eddie and Well'ard staggered out of the blast, took to their heels and ran, stumbling, coughing, desperate to get away from whatever was down in the Labyrinth. Eddie tripped over something, and fell, shrieking . . . and landed on something soft.

The something soft was Well'ard.

Eddie blinked and looked about. They were both sprawled in the middle of a scattered pile of toilet rolls. Somewhere in the corner a mop fell over with a clatter.

They were back in the caretaker's store.

The door stood slightly open.

Eddie licked his lips. "Claire?" he called softly.

Well'ard sat up, dislodging toilet rolls. "Where are they?"

"I dunno." Eddie called again, louder this time. "Claire? Stacey?"

But there was no reply. Eddie and Well'ard had staggered out of the Labyrinth alone.

Of the girls, there was no sign.

Chapter Nine
What a Drag!

"ALL RIGHT, WHERE is she?"

Andy folded his arms and glared at Eddie and Well'ard.

"Who?"

"Perce! She put you up to this, right? 'Go and tell Andy some old rubbish an' we'll have a good giggle', right?" He peered over their shoulders, looking for Perce's hiding-place. "She's going to jump out and yell 'Gotcha!', right?"

Eddie gave Well'ard a helpless look. They had rushed from the cellar straight to Andy's house and poured out the whole story.

"It's true!" yelled Well'ard. After a lifetime of telling porkies, and usually being believed, he was now telling the truth and being accused of lying! How unfair could life get? "We did see it, the tunnels an' the torches an' the pictures an' everything!"

Andy stared hard at him. Written on Well'ard's face was something that Andy had never seen there before: honesty. Usually when Well'ard told a lie, he looked too innocent. What's more, he really was scared stiff; and Well'ard wasn't scared of *anything*.

Andy humphed. "Why come to me about it?"

"We thought that you could . . . er . . . tell us what to do," explained Eddie.

"You should ask Perce," said Andy bitterly. "She's the expert on mythical monsters." He tried to shut his front door. Well'ard got his foot in the way and grabbed Andy's shirt front.

"Lissen," snarled Well'ard. "It's true, the laby-thingy is there. We were there in it, an' the girls *did* disappear. An' what about Syreeta an' Pete an' the others? How d'you think they feel about bein' chased through tunnels by a dirty great mad bull?"

"I should think it'd put them right off roast beef," said Andy.

Well'ard seethed. "OK, wise guy, let's go and see Perce."

"What if I don't want to come and see Perce?" enquired Andy loftily.

"You really that fond of hospital food?"

Andy choked. "I'll just go and get my coat."

Andy sat gazing out of the window. They were in Perce's lounge. Eddie and Well'ard were running through their story again, making slightly more sense this time. Andy still didn't believe it.

"We were well scared," finished Eddie.

"*You* were scared, I wasn't," snapped Well'ard.

"You said you nearly filled your pants, and you weren't talking about putting on weight." Well'ard gave Eddie a 40,000-volt look.

Perce's eyes were alight with excitement and she was nearly bursting with the effort of not yelling "Told you so!" at Andy. "Never mind about who was scared! I think I've found out what O'Taur's up to."

She told them what she'd read in the library. Even Andy began to take an interest as Perce related the story of Theseus entering the Labyrinth with the help of Minos's daughter, Ariadne. All three boys particularly enjoyed the outcome of the story: the single combat between Theseus and the monster in the echoing depths of the Labyrinth, and the hero's defeat of the Minotaur.

"Anything else?" asked Eddie when Perce had finished.

"Nothing important," Perce lied. She thought it best not to tell them about the bull dance. There was no point in scaring them into fits.

Andy was still not convinced. "If it's true, then why aren't you all in the Labyrinth now?" he demanded. "You've all been down there, so why didn't it capture you?"

Eddie was stumped and Well'ard didn't understand the question, let alone know the answer. It was left to Perce.

"I think it's all to do with the tribute – seven boys and seven girls." Andy looked puzzled. Perce carried on. "There are already seven boys in the Labyrinth: Pete and the six who helped O'Taur put away the vaulting-horse. So it doesn't need any more boys – that's why Eddie and Well'ard got out. But there's not enough girls. Only Syreeta, and now Claire and Stacey."

"So why didn't you get taken, if girls are needed?" asked Andy, still trying to pick holes in Perce's theory.

"I didn't actually go inside the Labyrinth, I

was sort of on the doorstep, still in the store-room."

Andy kept quiet. It seemed to make sense and he couldn't think of anything else. It was left to Eddie to ask the question they had all been avoiding.

"So if the Labyrinth only lets girls in, how do we get in there?"

A slow, evil smile crept across Perce's face. He watched it in alarm. "Oh, no! Perce!" Andy tried to hide behind the sofa. "Don't even think about it . . ."

Perce's eyes glinted. "To make the legend work, the Minotaur needs four more girls. Me and you three . . ."

A look of horror spread over Well'ard's face. "No way," he growled.

"We'd look stupid," protested Eddie, who was still wearing his matador costume.

Perce stared at him and raised her eyebrows. "Do you know how stupid you look *now*?"

"Anyway," protested Andy, "even if this

Labyrinth does exist, and we do get in, what happens then?"

"We defeat O'Taur and rescue everyone," said Perce matter-of-factly.

"Oh, that's all right then. Such a brilliant plan is bound to work," sneered Andy.

"I ain't going anywhere dressed as a girl," announced Well'ard.

By now Perce was desperate. She knew if she could convince Well'ard, the others would follow. "But, Well'ard, they're not girl's clothes really," she coaxed. "They're a disguise." She had an inspiration. "Like the SAS wear."

Eddie perked up. "Yeah, like in the war. Prisoners were always dressin' up as nuns to escape. Well-known fact."

"Like the SAS," said Well'ard, eyes wide open.

"Like the SAS," nodded Perce.

"Right, we'll do it!"

"Well'ard!" howled Andy. "Nooo . . .!"

Chapter Ten
All Strung Up

THE SIGHT OF Eddie, Well'ard and Andy walking towards school, dressed in Perce's clothes, caused several people to stop and gawp. Cats fled as they approached; mothers snatched their toddlers off doorsteps. A passing bus driver nearly wrapped his Number 47 round a lamp-post.

Well'ard had chosen a slinky top, with a pair of leggings. Both were black ("So I can't be seen in the tunnel"). They went well with his Doc Marten boots and a set of fluorescent-pink love beads Perce's mum had worn when she was a Sixties flower child.

Eddie tottered behind in an old flowery dress that Perce's grandmother had bought her (and Perce had refused to be seen dead in), and a pair of Perce's old wedges.

"How do girls walk in shoes like this?" he muttered, as he staggered sideways and twisted his ankle for the fifth time in as many minutes. He shifted his school-bag on to the opposite shoulder. He'd insisted on bringing his matador costume along. "After all," he had said, "you never know."

Perce grinned as she eyed Andy. "You look *ever* so nice."

"Just don't make any comments, OK?" Andy was wearing a pair of leggings with black-and-white horizontal stripes and a matching baggy T-shirt.

"I look like a bar code," he moaned.

"You look very fetching," cooed Perce.

"I'm warning you . . ."

The school gates were locked, so they had to climb over the wall, which provided some amusement for Perce, but not for Eddie in the dress.

"Why do you wear things like this? They're not practical!" he cried as he attempted to stop the dress blowing over his head. Perce turned away. Eddie's stick-insect legs and Mickey Mouse boxers were not a pretty sight.

Well'ard kept watch while the other three sprinted across the yard and down the steps to the cellar door. He needn't have bothered, the school was deserted.

"Right, here goes," whispered Perce as Well'ard joined them.

Steeling herself, she flung the door open.

They all stood and gaped. Beyond the buckets and mops, ghostly stone tunnels led off into the distance. Murals danced in the ickering torchlight. Deep in the tunnels pulsed a strange red glow.

"Sorry, Perce," said Andy in a small voice.

Perce nodded.

"Right, let's do it!" Well'ard pushed his way past the others towards the Labyrinth. As he stepped forward, the stone tunnels became less fuzzy and more solid.

"It's working. It's letting us in," Eddie cried out excitedly. He began to step forward.

"Wait!" ordered Andy. "How do we find our way out again?" Three pairs of eyes turned expectantly towards Perce. She had the answer.

"The same way Ariadne helped Theseus escape. She gave him a ball of string. He tied it at the entrance of the Labyrinth and unwound it as he went along, so when he wanted to get out, all they had to do was follow the string."

"And have you brought any string?" asked Eddie.

Perce shook her head. "Andy has, though.

He's always got string in . . . his . . ." She tailed off.

"Great!" Andy threw his hands in the air. "Yeah, I always keep string in my pockets, only my pockets are in my jacket over at your house, and here I am, thanks to your big idea, looking like a —"

"There must be some in here," interrupted Perce. "There's bound to be some string in a caretaker's store."

But there wasn't. Luckily, Eddie had a brainwave.

"What's soft, strong and incredibly long?" he asked.

"Your nose," suggested Perce.

"No — this." He held up a roll of toilet paper.

"Brilliant!" cried Perce. "Eddie, sometimes you're a genius."

Eddie beamed.

"But usually you're a div," said Andy.

★

As the four of them made their way through the tunnels of the Labyrinth, Eddie unwound the toilet roll behind them. He'd tied the end to the cellar doorknob.

The painted bulls followed their progress through the stone tunnels.

Andy looked at the bulls. He shivered as a sound that might have been a distant roar echoed through the tunnels. He wiped sweat from his forehead. The roar and the heat – all as they'd said. Next time he'd believe Perce – maybe. Still, he told himself, it might not be anything to do with O'Taur.

"What's that!" Well'ard's shout caused everyone to stop.

"I don't know."

"I heard something."

"So did I," yelled Eddie.

"RUN!"

The four of them shot off down the tunnel, Eddie leading the way, left, right, forward, twisting and turning through the Labyrinth.

"STOP!"

The four of them ground to a halt.

"Why are we running?" asked Perce, gasping for breath.

"Well'ard said we should," replied a wheezing Eddie.

"I didn't!"

"Did!"

"Stop bickering!" ordered Perce. "It's nothing. We just panicked. All we've got to do is go back to where we were. Follow the loo paper."

"Ah," said Eddie. There was a pause. "You know this paper is supposed to be soft, strong and incredibly long?"

"Yeah?"

"Well, two out of three ain't bad. It's soft and incredibly long, but . . ."

He raised his arm to show the others.

The toilet roll had snapped.

Chapter Eleven
The Bull Dance

THEY TRUDGED ON through the maze of tunnels.

There was nothing else to do. They had long ago lost all trace of the way out. At first, they had hunted high and low for the loose end of toilet roll, but finally had to admit that for all they knew, they could have been moving further away from it rather than towards it the whole time.

The tunnels seemed to go on for miles, with

the flickering torches set along them at intervals. On every wall, painted bulls charged; but as they looked more closely, Andy, Well'ard and Eddie could see that there were pictures of people on the wall, too. They were slim and strong, dressed in short kilts and tunics. They ran around the bulls, and . . . seemed to be flying over them.

Well'ard nudged Perce. "'Ere, what they doin'?"

Perce was looking straight ahead down the tunnel. "Who?"

"Them. In the pictures."

"Er . . . dunno . . ."

Perce's tone of voice made Andy's ears prick up. "What is it you don't want us to know about?" he asked.

"You don't want to know about it."

"Come on, Perce." Andy planted his feet and folded his arms. "Give."

Perce stopped dead, and sighed. "OK, OK." She sat down with her back against one wall of the tunnel. Andy sat opposite her. Eddie sat on his school-bag. Well'ard stood.

"The people in Crete called it the bull dance. It's what happened to the seven boys and seven girls that Athens sent to the Minotaur as tribute."

"They made them dance round the bull?"

"Not exactly *round*. More sort of . . . *over*. More sort of . . . *on*."

Well'ard sat down too; his legs had started to feel all wobbly.

"Are you saying they used to dance with the bulls?" Andy was aghast.

"Look at the walls."

The pictures suddenly looked menacing. Once they'd heard Perce's story, it was clear what was going on. The human figures were boys and girls, jumping over the bulls.

"You know that stuff O'Taur had us doing, with the horse? And the handlebars?"

"Look, they're . . . they're *vaulting*." Eddie's shaking finger traced the patterns of the leaping figures. "They're doing vaults over a socking great bull . . . and they're using the horns as *handgrips*!"

Andy shook his head in sheer disbelief. "Perce, it's not possible. Nobody could jump over a charging bull, it can't be done."

"OH, BUT IT CAN!"

The huge, deep voice echoed up the tunnel. Perce, Eddie, Well'ard and Andy gave each other one horrified look, and screamed.

The tunnel *tilted* beneath them. Scrabbling with hands and feet, they were tipped inexorably down as the slope increased. Gusts of hot air buffeted them, their ears were full of roaring, and they tumbled headlong into the red glow that rose from the depths to engulf them.

They landed in a crumpled heap. After a few seconds' groaning, they looked cautiously about.

They lay in a great cavern. The air seemed

to burn and throb. To their right, stood a massive stone slab. A huge bull's head was carved into the rock wall above it

To their left, a great stone throne rose out of the rock. In it sat a terrifying figure; powerful muscles glistened in the fierce red glow. The creature on the throne, though human from the neck down, had the shaggy head and curving horns of a monstrous bull.

"**Welcome**," rumbled the Minotaur.

Perce felt her stomach churn with terror. If you looked closely, she thought, you could see that the Minotaur was Mr O'Taur, in the same way that you could see a family likeness between a dachshund and a Dobermann; it was just that the Dobermann was a lot bigger and fiercer and very much more likely, if you tried to pat it, to have your arm off. She gave Andy a sidelong glance.

"There's your pal O'Taur," she whispered. "Still think he's the greatest?"

Andy looked sick. "Isn't it funny how you

can go off people?" Then he pointed. "Perce, look!"

On the other side of the cavern, standing as if in a trance, were Pete, Syreeta and the others; Claire, Stacey, the boys from the gym club. They were all dressed in loose kilts and tunics like the figures on the tunnel walls. Instantly, Perce's anger returned. She swung to face the monster on its great carved throne.

"What are you going to do to them?" she demanded.

"**You would do better to ask**," the Minotaur boomed, "**what I am going to do to *you***."

He — or *it*, thought Perce — stepped down from the throne and walked towards them. The floor shook. Eddie and Well'ard made a spirited attempt to back right through the solid rock. The Minotaur towered over the struggling figures.

"**You will join me in the bull dance, you and your friends**." The creature gestured towards its captives. "**You have been pre-pared for this**."

Perce shook her head. "No."

The monster threw back its horned head and laughed until stones fell from the cavern roof. "**Do you believe you have any choice?**"

"But Theseus killed you!" Andy's yell of defiance brought the great head swinging round to him.

"**Theseus banished me**." The roaring voice was dulled. "**He blocked the doorway from your world to my Labyrinth. But the wall between the worlds is thin, here. Another of my kind showed me a way through**."

"Ms Dusa," whispered Perce. So she had been right about a doorway between the worlds. Hooray.

The monster nodded. "**We are the children of the gods, we creatures of myth. Do you think you can defeat one of us and** not be called to account? **After all**," the cruel lips curled into a smile, "**we monsters must stick together**."

The creature raised its arms. "**You will all dance. Seven and seven will dance to the glory of the Minotaur**."

"Ah, yes, but . . ." gabbled Eddie, ignoring the filthy looks he was getting from Perce and Andy, "there's supposed to be seven boys, yeah, and seven girls, right . . ."

"Only we're boys really," added Well'ard, "so it wouldn't be proper, us dancin' on bulls 'cos we're not girls, we're . . . boys . . ." He tailed off.

The Minotaur moved in front of Well'ard. It thrust its great horned head down until its terrible breath made Well'ard's eyes water.

"**Tell you what**," it said, "**let's pretend**."

Chapter Twelve
A Red Rag to a Bull

PERCE STOOD FACING the monster with Andy, Well'ard, Eddie and the other blank-faced captives behind her. Trying to keep her voice steady, she asked, "What happens now?"

"**We dance**." The Minotaur nodded its great head. "**You must be swift and sure, for if you falter, you will be trampled to death**."

"And if we get through the dance without falling?"

"**Then you will be sacrificed on my altar to the greater glory of the Minotaur**."

"That's not fair!" protested Andy. "If we can't escape either way, why should we dance to suit you?"

"**Because you will not throw your life away. You will cling to it as long as you can, though you know what the end must be**."

Before their eyes, the Minotaur began to change. Its back humped. It fell on to all fours. The glossy hair of its head spread along its arms and down its back.

Where the Minotaur had been, there now stood a gigantic bull.

Andy gulped. "That's a good trick if you can do it."

Perce watched the monster closely. "It's part man, part bull. We've seen it turned into a man, we should've known it could turn into a bull as well."

The bull pawed the ground. Its defiant roar shook the cavern.

Andy looked at Perce and sighed. "You dancin'?"

"You askin'?"

"I'm askin'."

"I'm dancin'."

The bull roared again, and charged. Perce raced to meet it.

Instinct took over. The sessions with the vaulting-horse paid off. Perce leapt for the lowered horns, backflipped, sprang lightly off the bull's broad back, somersaulted and landed running. The bull turned.

The others were now coming into the fray. Andy faced the next charge, and a leap and a handspring took him over the bull's back. Well'ard followed. Eddie's clumsy spring left him sprawling, but the bull thundered on. Still in a trance, Pete, Syreeta and the others moved apart. The bull charged each in turn. They vaulted over it. The vaulting fell into a rhythm. Perce sprang, flipped, somersaulted again and again. The rhythm became a dance.

Gradually, Perce became aware that the bull moved slightly faster on every charge. At first, it had seemed easy — even exhilarating — to fly over the enormous, deadly creature in a perfect vault. But the vaulters were having to move faster every time, and make more complicated springs to avoid the bull's tireless rushes. The vaulters were not tireless. What had started almost as a game was now a test of endurance. The bull wasn't playing with them any more. Perce's arms were aching, her feet were like lead. All around her, heads were drooping. The bull dance, complex and beautiful though it was, was a dance of death.

Perce saw Syreeta stumble, and twist aside in the nick of time. Someone's not going to make it, she thought; someone's going to be trampled to bits. And it's going to be soon. For a moment, she almost despaired. Then, from some hidden ember of defiance inside herself, a sudden flame blazed. She ran to the edge of the cavern, grabbed Eddie's discarded school-bag, and fumbled it open.

Andy joined her, panting. "I don't think I can do this much longer."

Perce's eyes gleamed. "You won't have to."

Leaving Andy speechless, she stepped into the centre of the cavern, carrying a roll of cloth. At the same moment, Eddie made a mistake. Always the least capable of the vaulters, he had missed his spring, and landed sprawling, winded and helpless. The bull turned, lowered its horns, and hurled itself forward to trample and gore its first victim.

Perce stuck two fingers in her mouth and gave a piercing whistle.

"Hey, *toro!*"

The bull skidded to a halt. It tilted its head as if questioning what it saw.

Perce flicked the cloth she was holding, and it unrolled. She stood facing the bull, waving the red cape from Eddie's matador outfit

"*Toro! Olé!*"

The bull lowered its head and charged. Andy held his breath.

Perce whipped the cape aside. The bull thundered past. Its hoofs scrabbled at the rock as it tried to turn. Perce sprinted across the cavern.

"Here, *toro!*"

Again, the bull charged. This time, it was ready for Perce's side-step, and almost caught her, but Perce was too quick. Again, she sprinted across the cavern, and had taken a new position before the bull turned.

The bull grunted. Now it was mad. Any trace of human intelligence had left it. It was an animal, and it wanted to kill. This time, it would not fail.

The bull charged. Andy watched with his heart in his mouth, as it bore down on the tiny, defenceless figure.

At the last possible moment, Perce flicked

the cape away. Andy gave a sudden yell of triumph! Perce's last move had taken her to a position just in front of the altar. Distracted by the cape, the enraged bull had failed to see its peril until it was much, much too late.

Still running at full pelt, the bull charged head first into the great stone altar. There was a sickening, crunching and splintering thud as horn, hide and bone met hard rock.

Andy punched the air. "Bull's-eye!"

Eddie whooped in triumph. "One hundred and eighteeeee!"

After that, things got a bit confused.

The floor trembled and great cracks ran across it. Stone slabs tilted beneath their feet. The walls quivered, and rocks fell from the cavern roof high above. The red glow of the Labyrinth blazed in fury; the heat was suddenly unbearable.

"It's an earthquake," yelled Andy.

"It's a cavequake," corrected Eddie.

Perce skipped sideways to avoid a falling

rock. "Whatever it is, we want to be somewhere else."

Claire and the others were looking round in
a daze, as if they'd just woken up from a night-
mare and found that reality was a lot worse.
Perce took Claire and Stacey by the arms. "Get
moving!"

Andy grabbed Pete. "Where?"

"Out!"

"Sounds good." Dragging Pete, Andy led a
stumbling charge towards the nearest tunnel
mouth.

The torches guttered and flickered as they
staggered past. The roar of the collapsing
Labyrinth, its dust and heat, pursued them as
they fled up the tunnel.

" 'Ere, did you do all that?" Well'ard asked
Perce. His brain clearly hadn't quite caught up
with events.

"I suppose so."

"Nice one!"

"The Minotaur said the Labyrinth was his

world," panted Perce, "so without him, it's falling apart."

"Is he dead, then?" asked Andy.

"I didn't stop to take his pulse! Shut up and run."

"We're going the wrong way," howled Eddie.

"Keep going!"

"We'll never get out," sobbed Stacey.

Perce and Andy did their best to keep the line moving, but everyone was bewildered and exhausted. People were dropping to their knees, slumping to the floor, giving up. Perce stared at them helplessly, and then a flutter of movement caught her eye. There was something white, waving in the blasts of hot air from the tunnel depths. She gave a cry of delight, and pounced on it.

Eddie stared. "What've you got there?" He looked more closely, and his eyes widened with delight. He elbowed Perce out of the way, and grabbed the end of a roll of toilet paper. "Oh, you beauty," he cooed, fondling it.

Claire gazed at him in horror. "He's stroking a loo roll!" she wailed.

"It's all right," said Perce nastily, "it's not against school rules."

"But *why*?"

"Because it's the way out! Come on!"

The school yard was crowded when they staggered out through the sagging cellar door and up the steps. There were all the kids who lived close to the school, who'd seen the clouds of dust belching out of the cellar and heard the roar of the collapsing Labyrinth. There were their mums and dads, one of whom had called the fire brigade. Fire officers were arguing about whether they were dealing with fire, flood or subsidence. The police were tying striped tape between things and shouting "Move along there."

A battered Renault squealed to a halt as Perce and the rest stood blinking in the evening light. Mr Latimer got out in his gardening trousers and bedroom slippers.

He surveyed the bedraggled group, taking in the shattered cellar door; Andy, Eddie and Well'ard's strange appearance; and the dust-stained Greek kilts and tunics of the others. His eyebrows climbed up his forehead.

"It had better be good," he said.

Perce sighed and sat down in a heap. "Over to you, Well'ard."

Well'ard turned to Mr Latimer. A look of absolutely transparent honesty spread over his face.

"Well, sir," he began to lie, "it happened like this . . ."

READ MORE IN PUFFIN

For children of all ages, Puffin represents quality and variety – the very best in publishing today around the world.

For complete information about books available from Puffin – and Penguin – and how to order them, contact us at the appropriate address below. Please note that for copyright reasons the selection of books varies from country to country.

On the worldwide web: www.puffin.co.uk

In the United Kingdom: Please write to *Dept. EP, Penguin Books Ltd, Bath Road, Harmondsworth, West Drayton, Middlesex UB7 0DA*

In the United States: Please write to *Consumer Sales, Penguin USA, P.O. Box 999, Dept. 17109, Bergenfield, New Jersey 07621-0120*. VISA and MasterCard holders call 1-800-253-6476 to order Penguin titles

In Canada: Please write to *Penguin Books Canada Ltd, 10 Alcorn Avenue, Suite 300, Toronto, Ontario M4V 3B2*

In Australia: Please write to *Penguin Books Australia Ltd, P.O. Box 257, Ringwood, Victoria 3134*

In New Zealand: Please write to *Penguin Books (NZ) Ltd, Private Bag 102902, North Shore Mail Centre, Auckland 10*

In India: Please write to *Penguin Books India Pvt Ltd, 706 Eros Apartments, 56 Nehru Place, New Delhi 110 019*

In the Netherlands: Please write to *Penguin Books Netherlands bv, Postbus 3507, NL-1001 AH Amsterdam*

In Germany: Please write to *Penguin Books Deutschland GmbH, Metzlerstrasse 26, 60594 Frankfurt am Main*

In Spain: Please write to *Penguin Books S. A., Bravo Murillo 19, 1° B, 28015 Madrid*

In Italy: Please write to *Penguin Italia s.r.l., Via Felice Casati 20, I–20124 Milano*

In France: Please write to *Penguin France S. A., 17 rue Lejeune, F–31000 Toulouse*

In Japan: Please write to *Penguin Books Japan, Ishikiribashi Building, 2–5–4, Suido, Bunkyo-ku, Tokyo 112*

In South Africa: Please write to *Longman Penguin Southern Africa (Pty) Ltd, Private Bag X08, Bertsham 2013*